JIM AT THE CORNER

JIM AT
THE CORNER

Eleanor Farjeon

Illustrated by Edward Ardizzone

London
Oxford University Press

Oxford University Press, Ely House, London W. 1

GLASGOW NEW YORK TORONTO MELBOURNE WELLINGTON
CAPE TOWN IBADAN NAIROBI DAR ES SALAAM LUSAKA ADDIS ABABA
DELHI BOMBAY CALCUTTA MADRAS KARACHI LAHORE DACCA
KUALA LUMPUR SINGAPORE HONG KONG TOKYO

ISBN 0 19 271056 7

*First published
by Basil Blackwell 1934
First published in
this edition 1958
Reprinted 1959, 1966, 1973*

Printed in Great Britain by Fletcher & Son Ltd, Norwich

Here's a shell
for the ear
of Virginia Bell,
too young to read,
too little to spell,
too small
and lately-born
to hear
a merman call
to her through a horn,
or a mermaid sing to
her what I tell
in the shell
I bring to
Virginia Bell.

CONTENTS

I

DERRY AND JIM

Jim sat at the corner of the street by the pillar-box, morning and evening, summer and winter, on an orange-box. He had sat there as long as Derry could remember; yes, he had sat there for a lifetime, Derry's lifetime, eight years long.

Derry lived in one of the tall red-brick houses in

Jim's street. Whenever Derry went out for his morning walk, there was Jim on his orange-box at the corner; and whenever Derry came back from his walk, there he was still. For all Derry knew, Jim sat there all night as well as all day, taking care of the street and everybody in it. As long as Jim sat at the corner, Derry felt that the street was as safe as houses.

What did Jim look like? He was old enough to have white hair, as shining as silk. His skin shone, too, like a brown polished table. His eyes were as bright as blue glass marbles. His hands were gnarled, and were generally clasped over the top of a short stout stick, which he held planted between his knees like the third leg of a stool. He always had a pipe in the corner of his mouth. Even when he hadn't any baccy to put in it, Jim kept his pipe between his teeth. His lips always smiled, and his eyes always twinkled, and when Derry said, 'Hullo, Jim! How *are* you?' he always answered, 'Me? I'm fine. And how's yourself?'

Derry knew Jim's clothes as well as he knew Jim. Sometimes he knew Jim's clothes even before Jim did, for Derry's father had worn the tweed hat and the grey flannel trousers before Jim ever saw them.

And the mittens he wore in cold weather had been
knitted for him by Derry's mother.

And Major Trumpet, who lived next door to
Derry, had given Jim his brown jacket and his old
briar pipe.

And Mrs. Pattern, who lived on the other side of
Derry, had given Jim his sea-green shirt.

And Polly the parlourmaid over the way had
given Jim his sea-blue handkerchief.

All the street looked after Jim.

Whenever Derry's father went by, Jim touched his hat and said, 'Good morning, Mr. Vane. *Our* hat, sir!'

Whenever Major Trumpet passed, he tapped his pipe, saying, 'Good morning, Major! *Our* pipe, sir!'

And whenever any other body in the street turned the corner, Jim would beam and say, '*Our* boots, sir!' '*Our* socks, sir!' '*Our* scarf, miss!'

So Jim became part and parcel, not only of the street, but of everybody who lived in it; scarcely anybody could turn the corner without feeling that a little bit of himself was sitting on the orange-box with Jim.

LITTLE BOY PIE

EVERYBODY liked Jim, but it was the children who loved him best. For the exciting thing about him was that, long before they were born, he had been a sailor. He knew all the places on earth, and all the weather in the sky. He could tell you a day ahead what the weather would be like. And

he had a wonderful way of telling it you, something like this:

'There's a storm blowing up! Ah, that minds me
of the big storm off Cape Horn, when I was Mate
of the good ship *Rocking-horse*!'

Or: 'There's a frost coming at last. You'll be able
to skate tomorrow, the ponds will be covered with
ice. Never shall I forget the time the *Rocking-horse*
struck an iceberg off Newfoundland.'

Or: 'Wind's on the way. Get home quick afore
it comes, Derry, and if it ketches you, just you hold
on to your feet!'

'Why, Jim?' asked Derry.

'Why? You don't want to get blown off
'em, to the top of that plane-tree there, do
you? I've been carried to the top of a tree afore
now.'

'What, a big man like you, Jim?'

'Ah, but when I was a little boy like you. And
'twasn't a plane-tree that time, but an elm-tree full
of black rooks' nests, and the rooks all trying to
caw the life out of me!'

'Tell me about it, Jim!'

Jim moved a few inches on his box, and when

Derry had clambered on the free corner, and was dangling his legs, told him about it.

One summer, when I was a small boy, I had to keep the birds out of the peas. The peas were wanted as food for the cattle, and if the birds had their way the cattle would go short in winter.

From break of day till dusk I sat in the field, and when the birds came near me to steal the peas I shook my rattle at them and sang:

> 'Fly, rascals, fly,
> Or I'll make you into pie!'

Maybe they knew what the words meant, and maybe they did not; but whether they did or not, they flew away at once. Then I felt like a hero who had won a battle. The rooks and the starlings were the foe I had put to flight.

But as often as they flew away, back they came again. It seemed as though they would not learn their lesson. I could not think why they kept coming back. It must be for some very strong reason indeed, a reason more strong than their fear of me. It made me angry to see them defy me, and again I shook my rattle at them, and sang my song. So all that summer the birds and I did not love each other.

There was one rook, a bold black chap, the biggest of the lot, who did not mind my rattle or my song. He stayed among the peas, eating his fill, till I came so near that I could all but touch him. If ever I did catch him, I said to myself, I would surely take him home to my mother to be made into a pie. Rook Pie would be a tasty dish, and no mistake!

I crept like a mouse up to the big black bird, and put out my hand to grab his tail. And at once, as though he could hear my very shadow moving, off he flew with a loud 'Caw-Caw!' for all the world as though he had the laugh of me. But, 'You wait, old chap!' I called after him. 'I'll have you yet!' And I shook my rattle again, and sang:

> 'Fly, rascal, fly,
> Or I'll make you into pie!'

One hot day, in the noon, when the sun stood at the top of the sky, I took my dinner out of a bag I had with me, and began to eat. It was the sort of food I liked: two big bits of bread, with a slice of cold bacon inside them. I had to open my mouth wide to bite right through them, and the taste of bacon in the middle of the bite seemed to me as nice as any food could be.

Each bite filled my mouth quite full, and I had to chew and chew before I was ready for the next one. This was hard work on a hot day, and maybe that was why in the middle of a bite my jaws fell idle, my head began to nod, and my eyes to close. Before I had half done my bread and bacon I was fast asleep.

When I woke up I was not in the same place at all. I was lying at the edge of a field that was full of as queer a crop as I ever hope to see. It wasn't beans, and it wasn't peas, and it wasn't grass, or corn, or roots of any sort. No, what grew in that field, if you'll take my word for it, was slices of bread and bacon blowing in the wind.

Dear me, how good they did smell to a hungry boy like me! As quick as quick, I ran into the field and took a bite out of a slice as it grew. But I had hardly begun to chew it up before I heard a loud flutter of wings, and a harsh voice sang:

'Fly, rascal, fly,
Or I'll make you into pie!'

B

There, in the middle of the field, was a great black rook, as big as a giant, it seemed to me, and I was but a little tot who did not stand as high as his tail. The rook was rattling his wings, and singing my own song at me; and when I saw how big he was I took to my heels and ran for dear life.

'I'll never go near *that* place again!' said I to myself.

But in a little while I began to feel my hunger anew, and in spite of the rook I just had to creep back, to try to steal another slice. This time I managed to snatch two bites before he came at me with his wings and his song, and I only got away just in time.

You might think that cured me for good and all from trying to go into the bread-and-bacon field; but when a boy wants his dinner as badly as I did, he forgets to be afraid; and so, for a third time I stole round the field, slipped in at a new place, and began to eat.

This time I got three bites down, and just as I was feeling that all was going well, down came the rook on me, quicker than rain in April, and before I could run he had the tail of my little coat in his beak.

Up he flew, up, up, up, till I thought he was going
to bump into the sun; but no, he only flew as high as
the top of an elm-tree, where his nest was swaying
in the wind. Such a great nest it was, as round and
as black as a pot. Inside sat his big black wife and his
little black family, and when they saw what he'd got
in his beak, they all began to caw so loud that I
could not hear myself think.

'Why, Daddy,' said the Mammy Rook, 'you
never mean to say you've caught that fat little
rogue who is always coming after the bread and
bacon?'

'That I have!' said Daddy Rook, 'and if you want to please us all, you'll make him into pie.'

'Little Boy Pie is a tasty dish, and no mistake!' said Mammy Rook; and all the baby rooks cawed with joy:

'Little Boy Pie! Little Boy Pie! Give me a slice of Little Boy Pie!'

'Hand him over, Daddy,' said Mammy Rook, 'and I'll turn him into pie in a jiffy.'

'Catch him then!' said Daddy Rook, and tossed me across the nest from his strong beak. But he tossed just a little too strong; instead of falling into the nest, I landed on the other side of it, and before Mammy Rook could seize me in her claws, I jumped! Yes, I jumped from the very top of that tall elm, and fell down, down between the leaves and branches, until at last I came to the ground with a bump.

When I opened my eyes, I was sitting in my own field, with my own bread and bacon in my hand, and the rooks all busy at it among the peas. I jumped up and swung my rattle, and sang my song at the top of my voice:

'Fly, rascals, fly,
    Or I'll make you into pie!'

Off they flew as quick as comets, and when they had gone I ate up my bread and bacon.

But now I knew why the birds came back again and again, in spite of me and my rattle. They came back because birds, like boys, are hungry. I must not let them eat the peas, for then the cattle would go short, but when I got home that day I went into my own bit of garden and made a place for the birds to come and eat. I got my mother to give me a bit of bread to crumble there every day, and I begged my father to bring me a coconut to hang up for the tits. I even saved bits of bacon fat out of my sandwich, and threaded them on strings, and hung the strings of fat between two twigs.

So, if I had to keep the birds off with one hand, I fed them with the other; if I frightened them out of the field, I invited them into the garden. After that it seemed to me that the birds and I were not quite such enemies as we had been. Even though the rooks and starlings scolded me, the robins and the tits became my friends.

III

THE GREEN KITTEN

'THERE's a fine new plaything then!' said Jim, as Derry came whizzing along the pavement on a light bright fairy-cycle.

Jim had seen Derry go down the street in all sorts of ways. First in his Nanny's arms, when he was carried. Later on in his pram, when he was wheeled. Then in a red

15

wooden motor-car, that he could steer for himself.
And now on this gay new cycle with the spidery
wheels.

'Daddy and Mummy gave it to me for my birthday,' said Derry. 'I'm eight today.'

'If I live to see the tenth of August,' said Jim, 'I
shall be eighty. Nobody'll give *me* a fairy-cycle!'
He chuckled a little at the notion.

'What would you like best on your birthday?'
asked Derry.

'A sight of the sea,' said Jim, 'that's what I'd like
better than anything else—a sight of the sea, blue,
green, or grey, and the smell of it in my nose.'

'I hope you will live to see eighty, Jim,' said
Derry.

'And I hope you will!' said Jim heartily. 'It's a
very good age to be. What else did you have?'

'Seven birthday cards, and a letter from my
granny with ten shillings in it, and an engine
from my uncle, and a book from my aunt, and a
mouth-organ from Nanny, and a kitten from the
cat. She had five yesterday, so she could spare me
one.'

'What colour was it?' asked Jim. 'Green?'

Derry burst out laughing. 'It's black with white paws. There *isn't* a green kitten.'

'Yes, there is,' said Jim, 'because I've seen one.'

'Where?' asked Derry.

'Under the sea,' said Jim, 'when I was a sailor.'

All the children in the street knew that Jim had been a sailor *on* the sea, but it surprised Derry to hear that he had been a sailor *under* it. He exclaimed, 'Have you really been under the sea, Jim?'

'Of course I have! What d'ye take me for? A land-lubber?'

Derry didn't know what a land-lubber was, but he thought he had better not take Jim for one, so he said, 'No, of course not. Tell me about the green kitten.'

'I caught it in my shrimping-net,' said Jim, 'on the beach at Pegwell Bay.' He paused.

'Do go on, Jim!' urged Derry, leaning his fairy-cycle against the pillar-post.

'Seeing it's your birthday, said Jim, 'I will. But I've got to do some remembering first.' He blew his nose thoughtfully for some time, and then began.

It happened when I was a boy. I felt the call of the sea, and ran away from the farm in Kent where I was born. Our farm was not far from the coast, and soon I came to Pegwell Bay, where the good ship *Rocking-horse* was riding at anchor.

The Captain saw me coming, through his tele-scope, and when I was near enough he called, 'Come here, boy!' He had a commanding sort of voice, so I came.

He looked me up and down, and said, 'My cabin-boy has just run away to go on a farm.'

'That's funny,' I said, 'because I've just run away from a farm to go for a cabin-boy.'

The Captain looked me up and down, and said, 'You'll do. What's your name?'

'Jim,' I said. 'What's yours?'

'Cap'n Potts,' he said. 'Well, Jim, we don't sail till tomorrow, and tonight I feel like shrimps.'

'Like shrimps?' I said.

'Yes, like shrimps,' said Cap'n Potts.

Now when he said he was feeling like shrimps, I thought Cap'n Potts meant he was feeling sad, or seedy, or something like that. But it turned out he meant just what he said, for he handed me a big shrimping-net, and said, 'Go and catch some.'

That was a job any boy would enjoy, be he cabin-boy or farm-boy. I kicked off my boots in a jiffy, and went shrimping among the pools on the beach. The pools were surrounded by rocks, and the rocks were covered with thick green weed, like wet hair, very slippery to the feet.

When I'd got a nice netful of shrimps, I took them aboard the *Rocking-horse* and Cap'n Potts said, 'Well done, Jim! You'll make a first-class cabin-boy, I see. Take them below to Cookie, and tell him to boil them for tea.'

I went below and found Cookie, and said, 'Please, I'm Jim the new cabin-boy, please, and please, Cap'n Potts says will you please cook these shrimps for tea?'

'Shrimps! said Cookie. 'Do you call *this* a shrimp?'

He plunged his hand into the net, and fetched up what looked like a little lump of rock smothered in green seaweed. But the little lump wriggled in Cookie's hand, the little lump arched its weedy green back, the little lump waved a weedy green tail, the little lump pricked up two weedy green ears, the little lump wrinkled its weedy green nose, and *spat*. Next thing, it jumped out of Cookie's big hands, and clawed its way up to my shoulder, where it sat rubbing its soft green head against my cheek.

The little lump was nothing less than a wee green Kitten, with eyes as pink as coral.

The next day, when *we* sailed, the Kitten sailed too, and before long it was the pet of the ship. But I was its favourite, and it always slept in my cabin. Being the cabin-boy, I had, of course, a cabin to myself.

Now that first trip of mine we did not seem to have the best of luck. Everything the ship could have the *Rocking-horse* had, like a child who has chicken-pox, measles, and mumps, one after the other. The *Rocking-horse* had hurricanes, and icebergs, and pirates, and thunderbolts. Once she was wrecked, and once she was becalmed.

It was when she was becalmed that *my* adventure happened.

Cap'n Potts was a restless man, and liked to be on the move. It gave him the fidgets when the ship got stuck like that in the middle of the sea, and one evening he came up to me and said, 'Jim, I feel like lobsters!'

'Never mind, Cap'n,' I said. 'Perhaps we'll get a move on tomorrow.'

'Perhaps we will,' said Cap'n Potts, 'and perhaps we won't. But whether we do or don't, tonight I feel like lobsters.' Then he handed me a lobster-pot, and said, 'Go and catch some.'

Then I saw what he meant, and I got into a diving-suit, tucked the lobster-pot under my arm, dived over the side of the *Rocking-horse*, and sank to the bottom.

There was I, just a little nipper, all alone on the bed of the ocean. And there I saw wonders, to be sure! Coral and pearl and golden sands, coloured sea-weed as big as bushes, sunfish and moonfish like red-and-silver jewels, anemones like brilliant beds of flowers, and a sunken ship painted with gold and vermilion, like the castle of a king. The only thing I didn't see was lobsters.

I was just wondering how to catch what wasn't there, when I found I was caught myself. The long arm of an Octopus had shot out and whipped round me like a rope; next thing I knew, I was lifted up and dropped down into the state-room of the gorgeous ship I mentioned.

There I found myself face to face with an angry
Catfish. She was the biggest Catfish you ever saw,
and on her head was a little coral crown. She kept
opening and shutting her mouth at me, and gog-
gling her eyes at me, as cross as two sticks, and I
couldn't think why.

'You seem upset, ma'am,' I said.

'Upset!' she snapped. 'I should think I am upset!
And on top of it all you must go and call me ma'am,
as though I hadn't a royal title of my own.'

'Tell me what it is, and I'll call you by it, ma'am,'
said I.

'There you go again!' she snapped. 'Where are your eyes, boy? Can't you see the crown on my head? I am the Queen of the Catfish, and I want my Kitten!'

'Your Kitten, ma'am-your-majesty?' said I.

'My Kitten, booby,' said she, 'that you caught in your shrimping-net. And till Cap'n Potts gives it me back, he shan't have his cabin-boy. As long as he keeps my Kitten, I'll keep *you*!'

'Who's to let him know?' I asked.

'You shall write him a letter,' said she, 'and I'll send it up by Octopus.'

With that she set me down in the ship's saloon, a very glorious room indeed, with golden plate and jewelled goblets on the tables, and hangings of rich leather on the walls. I took off my diving-suit, pulled out my notebook and pencil, and scribbled a note to Cap'n Potts. This was it:

'Dear Cap'n Potts,

The Queen of the Catfish wants her Kittenfish, which is the green Kitten we've got aboard the *Rocking-horse*, and she's going to keep me till she gets it, so if you want me back send down the Kitten by Octopus, but if you'd rather have the Kitten than me, don't bother. I hope you are well, as this leaves me.

Yours obediently,
Jim.'

Just as I scribbled 'Jim', the Queen of the Catfish looked up and said, 'Is your letter done? The Octopus is ready to start.'

'Here's the letter, ma'am-your-majesty,' said I, 'but I'm afraid the pencil won't stand salt water.'

'We'll put it in a shell to keep it dry,' said the Queen of the Catfish. The saloon was littered with junk of all sorts, and she picked out a big spotted shell with a mouth like a letter-box. Then she posted my letter in the shell, gave it to the Octopus, and he went aloft.

I wondered a bit whether Cap'n Potts would rather keep the Kitten than have me back again. I would in his place, and I made ready to stay under the sea for the rest of my life. It wasn't a bad place to stay in, but I preferred the *Rocking-horse*. So when the Octopus came down again with the Kitten in its tentacle, I felt quite light-hearted.

It was a pretty sight to see that little green Kitten leap into its mother's fins, sea-mewing with pleasure; and the Queen of the Catfish was so pleased to see it that she turned from snarly to smiley.

'Get into your diving-suit, Jim,' she said, 'and my respects to your Captain, and tell him the next time he catches a Kittenfish he must throw it back, or there'll be trouble.'

'There *was* trouble,' said I, 'what with hurricanes, icebergs, pirates, and all.'

'Those were my doing,' said the Queen of the Catfish, 'but from now on you shall have fair winds and smooth sailing. Here's your lobster-pot.' With that she handed me my pot, and it was full to the brim with lobsters. 'Nasty vicious things!' said she. 'Always nipping my kittens when they get the chance. I'm glad to be rid of a few. Good-bye, Jim.'

'Good-bye, ma'am-your-majesty,' said I.

'Booby!' said she.

The Octopus took me in one tentacle, and the lobster-pot in another; the Kitten waved its paw at me, and the Queen of the Catfish kissed her fin, and up we went. In another moment I and the lobsters were put down safe and sound on the deck of

c

the good ship *Rocking-horse*, and wasn't I glad! I'd never thought to see her more.

Cap'n Potts was sorry to lose the Kitten, but when he saw the lobsters he said, 'Well done, my lad; you're an A-One Cabin-boy, *you* are!' Then the wind began to blow, and the sails began to fill, and the *Rocking-horse* was well under way when we all sat down to hot lobsters for tea.

And now see here what I've got in my pocket. It's the very shell I posted my letter in. I found it lying about the deck a few days later, and I've kept it ever since. It's a good shell, and a pretty shell, and seeing it's your birthday you can keep it, as a present from Jim. Put it to your ear, and you'll hear the sea in it. But don't go putting it to your Kitten's ear, or she might turn green—and then there *would* be trouble.

IV

THE ISLE OF PLENTY

HERE was a bit of a mist hanging about the street as Derry turned the corner one November day. He stopped as usual to talk to Jim, but Jim said, 'Now you run along home, like a good boy, before you get fog-in-the-throat.'

'All right,' said Derry. 'Good-bye till tomorrow.'

'Good-bye,' said Jim, 'till the day after the day after tomorrow.'

'Why, Jim? Won't you be here?' asked Derry.

'*You* won't,' said Jim. 'There's such a fog blowing up that I don't expect to see you under three days. Not if I know your Nanny!'

Jim was, as usual, right about the weather. The next day the fog was so thick that you couldn't see your hand before your face. It was in fact three days before Derry's Nanny let him go out for his walk again. He went straight to Jim's corner, and there was Jim on his orange-box.

'What did I tell you!' said Jim.

'I suppose,' said Derry, 'that the fog was the very thickest fog you ever saw, wasn't it, Jim?'

'Not it,' said Jim, 'by a long chalk!'

'But there couldn't be a thicker fog, Jim! When I looked out of the window, I couldn't see anything that was there!'

'Ah,' said Jim, wagging his head, 'but that's nothing to a fog when you can see what *isn't* there. Wait a bit, and I'll tell you!'

He made room for Derry on the orange-box, and after a moment or two, began.

It was after I'd become a grown man. We were coming home in the *Rocking-horse* from a trip to Jamaica. After a long voyage it's good to think about getting home, and that's what *we* all thought about, from Cap'n Potts down to me.

Now, on November the thirtieth, just as we got into Bristol Channel, we ran into a fog. It was so thick that it was like running into a black blanket. All round us foghorns were blowing from ships we couldn't see, and we blew our horn too, for they couldn't see us.

But worse than that, we couldn't even see our own ship. Although we were aboard of her, not one bit of the *Rocking-horse* could we see: neither larboard nor starboard, not a binnacle nor a spinnacle.

And worse than *that,* we couldn't even see ourselves! We all went stumbling round the decks, bumping into each other. When we bumped, we called, 'Who's there?' But we never heard the answer to our call. The fog was so thick that the sound of our voices couldn't get through. It was like trying to talk through the wall.

Ah, that *was* a fog! You couldn't tell the Captain from the cabin-boy, except by the feel of him.

Cap'n Potts was tall and thin, the cabin-boy was little and round. Anybody had the right, of course, to feel the cabin-boy all over; but it doesn't do, mind you, to go feeling your Captain! I got him once by accident, and knew him by the wart on the side of his nose. When I felt that, I dropped him pretty quick, and sheered off. He was a fussy man and might have had me put in irons for disrespect.

I felt like a lost man in that fog. I couldn't tell day from night, I couldn't find my bunk to go to bed in, or the cook's galley to mess in. It went on for days and days and days, just like that.

Well, one night or day (for in the fog I couldn't tell), I was feeling my way about, and put my arms round something long and lean. At first I thought it was Cap'n Potts again, and then I found it was the mainmast. For want of something better to do, I climbed up it.

When I got to the top where the flag was flying, it was like switching on the electric light in a dark room. All in a moment I was out of the fog, and into the sunlight. Everything under me was hidden by the fog, as black as a ploughed field in Novem-

ber. And all over me was blue sky and golden light,
and little bits of clouds as white as wool.

First I looked up, and stared at the blessed sun till
my eyes watered. Then I looked along, and rubbed
my eyes dry to make sure they weren't deceiving
me. For there, about half a mile away, floating on
top of the fog, was an island. A green island, with
flowers growing to the edge of the foggy sea, and
tall waving trees, and fountains playing. In the
middle of the island was a hill, and on top of the

hill was a palace, white and shining, with a dome like a diamond.

I said to myself, 'That's the place for me!' The fog looked as solid as the floor of a room, and I put out my foot meaning to walk across it. Next thing I knew, I found myself in the fog up to my neck, swimming in it for all the world as though it were the sea. The only difference was, that it tasted a lot nastier, when you got a mouthful by mistake.

As I got near the island, I saw a crowd of people on the shore, all watching me. In front stood a very tall man, in a red-and-blue robe like a parrot, and by his side was a beautiful girl in a silver dress, and behind them were two or three hundred other people, all in gay clothes. But the Parrot-Man and the Silver Girl were the only two I noticed particularly.

Well, I waded ashore, and began to squeeze the fog out of my hair; but the Silver Girl took me by the right hand, and the Parrot-Man took me by the left hand, and cried, 'Hail, King of Plenty!' Then they kissed my hands, and the crowd shouted, 'Hurrah!'

So I asked them, 'What's the matter?'

The Parrot-Man answered, 'This is the Isle of Plenty. There is everything here that the heart of man can want. Plenty of food, plenty of drink, plenty of flowers and fruit and fun—and you shall be King of it all!'

'Oh, then,' said I, 'you haven't plenty of kings?'

'Yes, we also have plenty of kings,' said the Parrot-Man, 'but we only have one at a time. We have a new king every moon.'

'What happens to the old kings?' I asked.

'Never mind that,' said the Parrot-Man. 'Come and be our king, and you shall see.'

They took me up to the palace on the hill, and sat me on a throne under the diamond dome. Then the Parrot-Man married me to the Silver Girl, and we sat down to a grand feast, the best I ever had in my life. There was boiled beef and carrots, pigs' trotters and pease pudding, pork pies and spotted dog, winkles and ice-cream cornets, kippered herrings and treacle roll, and I don't know what all. Then we had minstrels, who sang and danced to banjoes and concertinas. Then I slept a bit. Then we went out donkey-riding. Then we ate some more. Then we sang some more. Then we went to sleep again.

Then we rode on the donkeys again. And then we ate some more.

This went on for a month, and if you'll believe me, at the end of the fourth week I was fair sick of it. I'd had my fill of eating and sleeping and doing nothing all day long; I began to want to do a turn of work. I wanted to polish a brass, or holystone a deck, or splice a rope, or shiver a timber or so. And I went and said as much to the Parrot-Man.

'I'm fed up with being a king,' I told him, 'if this is all it comes to.'

'It's all it comes to on *this* island,' said the Parrot-Man, 'and as soon as our kings get fed up with their job, *we* get fed up with our kings.'

'What happens then?' I asked.

'Why, then,' said the Parrot-Man, 'we feed them up with a farewell dinner that lasts all day and all night.'

'What happens *then*?' I asked again.

'They burst,' said the Parrot-Man.

I looked at him to see if he was joking, but he wasn't. All he said was, 'I don't know how it is. None of our kings like it for more than a month. Well, I'll go and see the cook about that dinner.'

He went away, and left me feeling very uncomfortable. It didn't seem good enough somehow. I began to have a hankering for Cap'n Potts and the good ship *Rocking-horse,* and I strolled down to the shore to have a look at her mainmast sticking out of the fog, with her flag flying.

Now as I looked, I saw that she was about twice as far away as she was when I left her. Instead of half a mile, there was a good mile between her and the island. By this, I knew she must be moving. And if she was moving, the fog must be clearing down below. And if the fog was clearing down below, away she'd sail to the Bristol Docks. And if I didn't manage to get to her before she sailed away into Bristol Docks, it was all up with me.

Even as I looked, the sea of fog seemed to be getting thinner. And just at that moment, the dinner-gong began to ring in the palace, like the bells of St. Paul's.

'It's now or never!' said I to myself. I tucked up my trousers and rolled up my sleeves, and took the plunge into the foggy sea. Next moment I heard a shout from the palace; they'd seen what I was after, and came tumbling down to the shore in their

hundreds, to stop me. I swam for all I was worth, and to my relief, the shouts got fainter and fainter. But not at all to my relief, the fog got thinner and thinner. I was afraid it would give way under me, before I could reach the *Rocking-horse*.

But I swam my strongest, and grabbed her flag, just as the fog gave out. I hauled myself up to the mainmast, and slid down it to the deck, where Cap'n Potts and all hands were mustered, staring up at me. And there, a stone's throw from the vessel, were the quays and docks of Bristol

City, with the bells of Mary Redcliffe pealing us home.

Cap'n Potts said to me, 'Where in thunder have *you* been all this time?'

'All what time?' I asked.

'This twelve hours of fog,' said he.

'This month of fog, you mean,' said I.

'Nonsense, my lad,' said Cap'n Potts, and he showed me the calendar to prove it. The fog had begun on November the thirtieth, and the calendar said December the first as plain as a pikestaff. There was no argufying with the calendar, so I just scratched my noddle, pointed aloft to the crow's-nest on the mast, and said, 'That's where I've been, Cap'n! sitting up there, keeping a look-out for sharks. Land ahoy, Mates!'

And we drew up alongside the quay, and stepped ashore.

Well, if I'd told the Captain the truth he'd never have believed me.

V

FLIP THE PENGUIN

HERE had been a heavy snowfall, and Derry, like all the other children, had gone up to the Heath, to slide on the frozen ponds, or swish down a long white slope on his wooden sled. It was like a new world on the Heath, soft and sparkling. Children laughed and tumbled and threw snowballs, dogs leapt and barked, and everybody was fresh and happy, and came home hungry to dinner.

For two days the snow lay thick, and the ice held. On the third morning the ponds were no longer safe; the sun had begun to melt it, and water splashed among the floating sheets of ice. On the slopes the snow no longer lay like a thick white blanket; it was all mussed up, and the brown earth was making it dirty. When Derry had a tumble he came up black now, not white, and he trotted home with a pair of grubby knees.

'You're back early today,' said Jim, as Derry reached his corner panting.

'Yes,' said Derry, sitting down for a rest on the orange-box; 'it isn't so nice on the Heath today as it was yesterday.'

'Ah,' said Jim, 'snow's all very well till it turns into slush. It's all very nice so long as it lies atop of the dirt; but later on, when you've kicked it about a bit, the snow and the dirt don't agree.'

'I wish I could kick it about as much as I liked *without* any dirt underneath,' said Derry.

'What *you* want,' said Jim, 'is to go to the South Pole, where it's snow from first to last.'

'I've got to be home for dinner in half an hour,' said Derry.

'Ah, 'twill take you more than half an hour,' said Jim, 'and when you do get there, you may get stuck fast in the ice, like the *Rocking-horse* did for a matter of three months.'

'Were you on the *Rocking-horse*, Jim?' asked Derry.

'I was that,' said Jim.

'Weren't you very lonely?'

'Not a bit of it! For one thing, there was Cap'n Potts and all the rest of the crew with me. And for another thing we had the penguins.'

'But penguins aren't people, Jim.'

'Aren't they? Then they're the next thing to it! There they were, hundreds and hundreds of them, all in black-and-white like so many little parsons, and behaving for all the world like little people. Very friendly little people, too. We got mighty fond of the penguins before we said good-bye. But to my mind, there was none of 'em to touch Flip.'

'Who was Flip, Jim?'

'Flip was my particular pet, and I was his. You see, in a manner of speaking I was his wife.'

Derry squeaked with laughter. 'You, Jim! Flip's wife!'

'I said *in a manner of speaking*, didn't I? That's how Flip the Penguin looked on me, and if you laugh like that you'll fall off the box. Do you want to hear about it, or do you not?'

'I do, please, Jim.' Derry stopped laughing at once, and sat quite still, while Jim told him about Flip.

First I must tell you that when penguins start looking for their sweethearts, they bring the lady penguins presents. What sort of presents? Ah, a very funny sort. They bring them stones. Stones to build their nests with. In that cold, hard land there's no grass or straw or wool, so the penguins build their nests of stones, just as a man might build his house.

The gentleman penguin sees some lady penguin that takes his fancy. Then he looks about for a nice big stone to make a start with, and offers it to her. If the lady penguin likes him, she takes the stone and begins her nest, but if she doesn't like him, she pecks him, as much as to say, 'Be off!'

Well, one day I saw Flip pushing a great big stone

D

along, and I said, 'Hallo, Flip; going courting?' And Flip flapped his flipper and winked at me with his little white eye, as much as to say, 'That's right, Jim!'

He rolled his stone up to a handsome bird we called Penelope, or Penny for short. But Penny wouldn't have it. She just gave Flip one hard peck, and sent him away.

Then he rolled his stone over to another fine bird we called Guinevere, or Gwynnie for short. And Gwynnie wouldn't have the stone, either. *She* gave him a peck and sent him packing, just like Penny.

Well, Flip looked so sad about it that I sang out, 'Poor old Flip! Better luck next time!'

Flip gave me just one look, and rolled the stone right across the ice to *me!* And there he stood looking up at me with his little white-ringed eyes, in a hopeful sort of way, as though he were asking: 'Will *you* have my stone, Jim? Please do!'

It wasn't in my heart to say him nay. I took the stone, and patted Flip on the head, and he flapped his flippers joyfully, and began to run about to get me a lot more. Before long we'd built, between us, the finest nest of stones on the ice-field. Penny and Gwynnie had chosen their mates by this time, and their nests weren't half so fine as ours. They looked pretty jealous, and sent their husbands to try to sneak some of our stones away. So I got out my jack-knife, and amused myself with cutting the letter F on every one of our stones, to show that they were *our* stones. F for Flip, you know.

Well, next thing Flip wanted was some babies, and he sat down and waited for me to lay him some eggs. But of course it wasn't in nature, and I had to disappoint him. To please him, I sat a bit on the nest every day, and he brought me tit-bits of fish for my dinner. Cap'n Potts and my mates stood round laughing at us. Then Flip waddled about flapping at them very fierce with his flippers. I wouldn't let them tease him, and he wouldn't let them disturb me. Oh, we were great friends, Flip and me!

Well, after a few weeks Cap'n Potts said, 'Mates, we haven't found that South Pole yet, so let's get a move on.

We packed up the sleds, and said good-bye to Penny and Gwynnie, and all the other little penguin people. When I said good-bye to Flip, I fairly

blubbed, and *he* piped his eye too. But it had to be. I left him sitting on our heap of stones, and I waved my handkerchief to him till we were out of sight, and he waved his flipper. Ah well, the best of friends must part! We d come all that way to find the South Pole, and not to hob-nob with penguins.

Maybe you want to know if we ever *found* the South Pole? Well, to tell you the truth, we found so many things that I can't remember now if that was one of them. But about a year later we did find the biggest iceberg man ever set eyes on. How big?

Oh, about a thousand times as big as the Tower of London. It took us all day to walk round it.

It was a most exciting iceberg! All the way round it was full of caves and caverns, gleaming arches and icy passages. Cap'n Potts wouldn't let us go too far in. I wanted to go right to the end of one of them. They were full of blue light, like sapphires and moonstones.

One day Cap'n Potts said again, 'Well, boys, to-morrow we must get a move on.' And that night I thought I'd go and explore one of the caves for my-self, because it was my last chance. I'd seen one with an opening like a horseshoe.

'That's the one for me!' I said to myself. 'Horse-shoes are lucky. Maybe there's some big treasure at the end of it, in the heart of the iceberg.'

I waited till my mates were asleep, and I slung my sleeping-bag over my shoulder, to bring back the treasure in. If I found it, I'd have the laugh of my mates, sure enough.

It was the time of the year when the night was as bright as the day. I found my horseshoe cave, and in I went.

The light came in with me, for a long way,

making the icy sides of the cave shine like walls of jewels. Then the cave began twisting and turning, and got me all topsy-turvy; and it was hard walking on the icy floor like frozen sea-waves, with cracks in between.

Then, just as I was thinking I d better give up the treasure hunt and go back, I slipped in one of the cracks and ricked my ankle. I couldn't walk, so I had to crawl. When I'd crawled for an hour, and didn't get out of the berg, it dawned on me that I was lost inside it. Yes, I might have been locked up in one of the dungeons in the Tower of London itself. Well, that was not nice. What did I feel like? The less said about that the better.

A long time went by. It seemed like a month, but maybe it wasn't more than a day. I knew my mates would never guess where I was, and if they did guess, who could ever find me in the heart of the iceberg? I lay inside my bag to keep warm, and got hungrier and hungrier. Sometimes I dozed off a bit.

I waked up out of one of my dozes to feel something patting my cheek. I looked up, and bless me if there wasn't Flip sitting beside me, peeping at me out of his round white eyes, and touching my face very gently with his flipper. Because a penguin's flipper is as hard as horn, and not feathers at all.

'Hallo, Flip!' I said.

Flip as good as answered, 'Hallo, Jim!' and dropped a bit of fish on the outside of my face. That bit of fish was very soon inside my face. Then I felt better, and went to sleep again. Every time I waked up there was Flip with another fish.

After about ten times I waked up and there was *no* Flip, only a whole heap of fish to show how often he had been and gone. I felt lonesome without him. I'd rather have had Flip than a hundred fish. However, I ate some, and when I moved I found that my ankle was better, and I could walk again. *That* was a good thing, anyhow.

I stretched myself a bit, and looked about, wondering which way to go. As I looked, what do you think I saw a little way off? What but a stone! I went up to it, looked a bit closer, and there on the top was a big F, carved with my own jack-knife. F for Flip! That stone had come from our own nest, and could only have been brought there by Flip.

It cheered me up no end, and before that nice feeling had stopped in me, I saw *another* stone! So I went up to that one, and sure enough it had an F on it too. And a little way off was a third stone.

Then I saw what Flip's game was. While I was asleep he had laid a trail of our nest-stones right from where I lay to the mouth of the cave. I'd no difficulty in finding my way out of the iceberg after that, and when I did get out I saw a long line of the stones stretching away over the snowfields. At the end of them was our camp, and half-way between was Cap'n Potts himself, coming to find me. He was following the stones from the other end.

When he saw me he gave a big shout, and ran; and I ran too.

'Hallo, Cap n!' I called.

'Hallo, Jim!' he called. 'How goes it?'

'Fine!' I shouted. 'How long have I been gone? Two years?'

'Two days!' he shouted back.

When we got near enough to talk properly, I pointed to the stones and said, 'I bet you my knife you don't know who did this.'

'Flip did it,' said Cap'n Potts. 'He came to our tents yesterday and kicked up a rare fuss, but we couldn't make out what he wanted.'

'Ah,' I said, 'he'd found me in the iceberg, and wanted you to come and haul me out.'

'That's right,' said Cap'n Potts, 'only we were too stupid to know it. So he went and laid this trail. Jim,' said Cap'n Potts, 'it's in times like this a man comes to know how much a man doesn't know, and how much more a bird knows than a man does.'

'Flip's no common bird,' said I.

I went back to camp, and had a good feed and another sleep. And next morning, the stones were all gone again.

You may think that was the end of it, but no!

On the way back we had occasion to pass the old

penguin country, at nesting time. What a fuss those birds did make of us! Penny and Gwynnie, and all the other mothers, came running to show us their new babies. But it was Flip who made a beeline for me—if a penguin can make a beeline. He flapped me along to the finest nest of the lot—it was all made of our own stones. On the top sat the handsomest female penguin you ever set eyes on, and under her breast the grandest little brood of penguin chicks.

And now just you listen to this. While I was praising Flip for his cleverness, Cap'n Potts called out, 'Jim, come here!' No sooner had he said it, than the finest of the little penguins pushed out from under his mother, and ran to see what the Captain wanted. By that I knew Flip had called his eldest son after *me*. Nice of him, wasn't it? So we all parted happy.

There's only one thing more. You remember I'd lost my jack-knife to the Captain, over that bet. He reminded me of that as we were sailing for home in the *Rocking-horse,* and of course I stumped up. But no sailor can ever be without a knife, so, to make all square, Cap'n Potts gave me his. And as luck would have it, it was a better one than mine.

VI

THE NINTH WAVE

DERRY had just come back from the seaside, as brown as a berry, after the Easter Holiday. He hadn't seen Jim for a month, so the next morning he ran to the corner to talk it all over.

'What did you do?' asked Jim.

'Oh, everything! I paddled, and I bathed, and I

can swim three strokes now, and I went shrimping, and got stung by a jelly-fish, and I had tea on the sands almost every day, and I found four agates, and went in a boat, and I've brought you this.'

And Derry gave Jim a long thick pink stick of Selsey Rock.

Jim took a suck, and then a bite, and said, 'Ah, you've had a rare good time. You're a proper seaman by now. Were you sick in the boat?'

'Not exactly,' said Derry.

'I know that not-exactly feeling, well,' said Jim.

'Do sailors have it too?' asked Derry, with some surprise.

'Lord Nelson always had it,' said Jim. 'Why, if it comes to that, I've known a codfish have it!'

'Some of the waves are *so very* big,' said Derry.

'That's just it,' said Jim. 'Especially the ninth wave.'

'Is that true, Jim?' asked Derry. 'A boy on the sands told me the ninth wave was always bigger than the others, but it was awfully hard to count them properly.'

'It may be hard off Selsey,' said Jim, ' but it's as easy as pie off Nova Scotia, as well I do remember.'

'When, Jim?' asked Derry.

'Bide quiet, and I'll tell you,' said Jim. Derry leaned against the pillar-post, and Jim sucked at his stick of rock for a moment or two. Then he told Derry the tale of the biggest wave he had ever met.

It was in the grey Atlantic, off Chedabucto Bay. We were fishing for tunny that trip. The seas ran high, and on the day I speak of, the *Rocking-horse* was pitching and tossing like a swingboat at a fair. There were more waves, and bigger waves, in the ocean that the ship knew what to do with. Cap'n Potts was a rare good captain, but every once in a while the *Rocking-horse* got a slap on the side that made her jump. And of course every ninth wave bumped her a bit more than the eight that went before.

I had that not-exactly feeling that day. So before I started fishing I took a dose of medicine, and kept the medicine glass and bottle handy, in case I wanted some more, for I saw there were still bigger waves to come. Then I let down my line. Cap'n Potts had offered a prize for the biggest tunny anybody caught. It was to be two ounces of baccy, so of course I wanted it badly.

For some time I had no luck at all. Then, just as a big ninth wave came rolling along, I felt a tug on my line, and hauled. Up went the *Rocking-horse* over the wave-top and up came my hook with a Codfish on it. I was fair disgusted, because when you're fishing for tunny, it's tunny you want. If I'd been fishing for cod, I wouldn't have minded.

I felt a bit sick about it, and I was just going to hit the Codfish on the head, when he said, 'Don't do that!'

'Why not?' I asked.

'Because I'm feeling poorly,' said the Codfish.

I looked him in the eye, and saw he was as sick as I was.

'Call yourself a fish!' said I. 'I wonder at you!'

'You need not, Jim,' said he. 'That last wave *was* a whopper, wasn't it now?'

'It was,' I said. 'And how d'ye come to know my name?'

'I hear them calling to you all day long,' said the Codfish. '"Jim," they say, "how shall we do this?" "Jim," they say, "how shall we do that?" "What

does Jim advise?" they say. I suppose,' said the Cod-fish, 'you must be the captain of this craft, mustn't you?'

'Well, not exactly,' I said. But of course I couldn't help feeling flattered; *this* not-exactly feeling was a nicer one than the other sort. I began to have a liking for the Codfish, and as he was still looking queer I fetched a lifebuoy. I propped up his head on it, and smoothed him out so that he lay more comfortable.

'Thank you, Jim,' said the Codfish.

'You're welcome, Claude,' said I. He looked like Claude, you know.

'Don't tell the Captain I'm here,' said he.

'I'll keep you dark,' said I, 'and as soon as the sea's a bit more peaceful, I'll throw you back.'

'You're a Christian,' said the Codfish, 'and if ever I can do you a good turn, I will.'

I didn't see just how a codfish *could* do me a good turn, but I knew he meant it kindly, and I took it in that spirit.

Well, before long the *Rocking-horse* got into that worse weather I'd seen ahead of her. The waves got bigger and bigger, they rolled up like green mountains one after another, and every ninth wave was bigger than ever. After one monster, I saw Cap'n Potts strolling up with his telescope to his eye. I threw my tarpaulin jacket over Claude and covered him up. I didn't want the captain to have him boiled for supper, d'ye see?

'Jim,' said Cap'n Potts, 'the weather's getting worse and worse.'

'And *worse,* Cap'n,' said I.

Said Cap'n Potts, 'If we get a bigger Ninth Wave than the last one, we're done.'

Said I, 'That's the truth, Cap'n.'

'What's more,' said Cap'n Potts, 'she's coming. I've just sighted her in my telescope, rolling up over the horizon. Now, Jim,' said Cap'n Potts, 'only one thing can save us.'

' Name it, Cap'n,' said I.

'Oil,' said Cap'n Potts.

You've heard of throwing oil on troubled waters, haven't you? It was Cap'n Potts' idea to pour all the oil we'd got left on that raging, boiling sea. But how much *had* we got left?

'Eight bottles,' said the Captain. And he put down a basket with eight pint bottles of the best olive oil, which we used for our salad when we had any, only being at sea of course we never did. So the oil could be spared.

'Now, Jim,' said the Captain, 'every time you see a wave coming, break off a bottle-neck and souse it with oil.'

'Right, Cap'n!' said I. 'Eight bottles will account for eight waves. And *what* about the Ninth?'

But Cap'n Potts had turned away to reef the jib, and didn't seem to hear me. So I knew I must do the

E

best I could with what I'd got, and then say my prayers.

Soon I saw the first wave of the new lot coming along. Before he could hit us I cracked the first bottle-neck, and threw the oil full in his face, so to speak. That wave sank down with a sort of sick look, like a balloon when you bust it. There was no more harm in *him*.

But I hadn't much time to rejoice, for along comes Wave Number Two. *Crack!* went the second bottle-neck; *glug-glug!* went the oil; and *biff!* went *that* wave, like the one before him. Right on his heels comes Wave Number Three.

Crack! Glug-glug! and *Biff!* as before. And so it was with Waves Number Four, Five, Six, Seven, and Eight. Five more *Cracks!* Five more *Glug-glugs!* and five more *Biffs!*

Then the oil was all gone, and I saw Wave Number Nine rolling up, the wave that was bigger than all the eight put together. He reared up like a dragon, curling his great green-and-white tips at us with a wicked grin, meaning to devour the *Rocking-horse* and all souls aboard. That seemed to me the time to say my prayers.

Just as I flopped on my knees I heard a voice say 'Jim!' It came from under my tarpaulin jacket, so I knew it was the Codfish speaking.

'Hallo, Claude!' said I. 'I'd forgotten all about you.'

'I hadn't about *you*,' said Claude. 'Just you look in the medicine glass.'

I turned back the tarpaulin a little, and there lay Claude, looking a trifle pale, I thought, and by him was the medicine glass I'd taken my dose in. It was full to the brim of oil—not olive oil, mind you, but a sort of oil that made me hold my nose.

'What's this, Claude?' I asked.

'It's cod-liver oil, Jim,' said Claude.

'Where did it come from?' I asked.

'My liver,' said the Codfish modestly.

'What's it for?' I asked.

'For the Ninth Wave,' said Claude.

I expect you've taken cod-liver oil, and I expect you know that if there's one thing worse than another, it's *that*.

I leaned over the side of the ship, and held up the medicine glass fair and square with my right hand, and held my nose with my left. And just as

that Ninth Wave towered over us, and prepared to topple, I threw the cod-liver oil full in its horrid jaws.

But not one drop of the oil did that wave swallow. When it saw what was coming, it just turned tail and *ran*. It ran as fast as a wave can run right to the horizon, and over the edge; and as it ran, it swept before it all the other waves that were coming along, leaving the sea as smooth as a window-pane. So smooth, in fact, that the *Rocking-horse* stood still with surprise.

I saw Cap'n Potts standing on the bridge, looking after the waves through his telescope. When they were all gone, he began to come down to me; but before he reached me I'd picked up Claude in my arms.

'Time to go home, mate,' I said, 'and thank 'ee kindly.'

'That's all right, mate,' sez he; 'one good turn deserves another.'

I kissed him good-bye on his cold, wet nose, and a tear fell out of his round, pearly eye. Then I slid him over the ship's rail, and saw his silver body shoot down into that green and glassy sea.

Up comes Cap'n Potts, and says, 'Well done, Jim! You've saved the ship.'

And for the life of me I couldn't tell him she'd been saved by a Codfish. Well, it didn't seem likely, did it?

VII

THE STAR THAT WATCHES THE MOON

ERRY's godfather had been to visit him, and before he went away he asked Derry what he would like for a present. Derry, whose mind was full of Cap'n Potts, said at once, 'A telescope!' So they went to the toyshop, and Derry's god-father bought him the best telescope to be had there.

There was one for a shilling, and one for three and sixpence, and Derry felt sure it would be the shilling one. He turned his head away, trying hard not to hope too much. When he heard his godfather say, 'That one, please!' he turned his head back again, and saw his godfather putting three shillings and sixpence down on the counter.

Derry was filled with joy, for now he was sure he would be able to put this best of telescopes to his eye and see ships and waves and whales and icebergs, just like Cap'n Potts. But when he looked along the street, he could still only see houses and cabs and horses and people and shops. Only they all looked a little different seen through the telescope. Sometimes they looked much clearer, and other times they did not. Derry went to Jim and asked him why this was.

'Ah,' said Jim, 'that's a fine little telescope, to be sure! If you don't see clear through it, it's because you don't get the focus right.'

'If I got it right, could I see the sea?' asked Derry.

'Not with all the houses in the way,' said Jim. 'But there's other things to look at through a telescope besides the sea. There's the sky. You take a good look at the sky tonight, before you go to bed.'

So Derry did.

'Well,' said Jim the next day, 'what did you see last night?'

'Well,' said Derry, 'I looked out of the window with my own eye, and I saw the Moon. Then I looked with the telescope and I saw the Moon and *one* star. Just one.'

'Rather near the Moon, was she?' asked Jim.

'Yes, quite near,' said Derry.

'I thought as much,' said Jim. 'That's the Star that watches the Moon.'

'What for?' asked Derry.

'I'll explain,' said Jim, 'when I've had three puffs of my pipe.' He took his three puffs, and then explained.

You know, of course, that this old world of ours has a sun by day and a moon by night. One moon, only one, but that's enough for us. We'd be badly off without her, naturally, but one moon is as much as any world wants.

But somewhere a long way off in the sky there's

another world called Saturn, a greedy old chap who has no less than seven moons. And even *they* don't satisfy him. He's always trying to get more.

Old Saturn he looks around the sky for what he can take, and when he sees something pretty he uses all his wits to get hold of it. One time he stole a ring of light, and put it round him for a body-belt. That's how he got those seven moons of his, stealing here a moon and there a moon whenever he saw a chance. Then one fine summer night his sharp eye spied *our* Moon shining away for all she was worth, and he said to himself, 'Eight moons are better than seven. I'll have her too!'

Now Saturn is fixed in his place in the sky, so he couldn't come himself to fetch her away. He called for a Shooting-Star and said:

'Hark ye to me! I want the Moon that shines upon the Earth, and you must go along and tell her so.'

'What if she won't come?' asked the Shooting-Star.

'Oh,' said Saturn, 'you must so sing in her ear that she *will* come.'

Off went the Shooting-Star across the sky, quicker than a drop of rain falls from heaven to earth. He made up his song as he flew, and when he came abreast of the Moon he sang it in her ear:

> 'Moon, go follow the pathway bright
> To Father Saturn in heaven,
> And you shall spin in a ring of light,
> With your sisters seven.
> You shall not play alone in the night,
> You shall make a silver pattern,
> And sing sweet tunes with the seven moons,
> That dance round Father Saturn.'

When his song was finished the Shooting-Star fell to Earth, for the life of such stars is as short as it is swift. But his song was quite enough to excite the Moon, who was but a young little thing, a mere slip of a crescent at the time. She began to try to wriggle her way across the sky to the House of Saturn, where she would no longer be lonely, but would spin in a ring of light with seven playfellows.

The moment she started, a shiver went through the Earth, who knew at once that something was wrong up aloft. So old Mother Earth sent for Mister Galileo.

This Mister Galileo was a very wise man; he knew all that anybody could know about the goings-on in the sky, and if anybody could explain things, he could.

He came along at once, and said, 'What's the matter *now*, Mother Earth?'

'Mister Galileo! Mister Galileo! I feel a shiver in my bones!'

'Are you going to have a quake, Mother Earth?'

'No, Mister Galileo! The shiver comes from outside me, not inside me. It isn't an earthquake, it's a skyquake, Mister Galileo! Something's moving up aloft where it has no business to be moving!'

'I'll have a look,' said Mister Galileo.

He got his big telescope and cocked it at the sky, and turned it slowly round. When he got to the place where the Moon ought to be, she wasn't there, but *there*—ever such a tiny bit out of place, but Mister Galileo spotted it at once, because he knew all.

'Well, Mother Earth, it's the Moon is the trouble. She is a little out of place.'

'Mister Galileo! Mister Galileo! If the Moon gets out of place I shall simply go to pieces. Oh, Mister Galileo, what are we going to do about it?'

'Let me think,' said Mister Galileo.

He put away his telescope, and went to walk in

his garden, with his hands behind his back. His garden was always in beautiful order, with the flower-beds and grass-plots and gravel paths just *so*. So that when in his walk he kicked against something hard, he knew it ought not to be there, and stooped to pick it up. He had a tidy mind, and did not like anything left lying about, whether it was a brick, a bit of blue china plate, or a garden trowel whose proper place was the tool-shed.

But the thing that had hurt Mister Galileo's toe was none of these. It was a lump of cold iron of a curious shape; and Mister Galileo knew at once that it was a shooting-star with its light out.

'Something more for my collection!' said Mister Galileo.

Before he put it away he examined it closely to find which drawer it ought to go in, and then he saw that it must have a drawer all to itself, for it was like no other cold shooting-star that he had ever seen. It was marked all over with sky-writing.

Mister Galileo could read sky-writing as easily as A B C, for Mister Galileo knew all. And this is what he read in sky-writing on the Shooting-Star:

'Moon, go follow the pathway bright
To Father Saturn in heaven,
And you shall spin in a ring of light,
With your sisters seven.
You shall not play alone in the night,
You shall make a silver pattern,
And sing sweet tunes with the seven moons,
That dance round Father Saturn.'

When Mister Galileo had read the poem through, he exclaimed, 'That explains it!' and he went back to Mother Earth as fast as he could go. She saw him coming, and cried:

'Mister Galileo! Mister Galileo! Have you found out what's the matter?'

'I have indeed, Mother Earth.'

'Is it something serious?'

'It is indeed, Mother Earth.'

'Alackaday! what can it be?'

'Father Saturn is trying to steal your Moon, Mother Earth.'

'Alackanight! what shall we do?'

'We'll stop his little game, Mother Earth.'

'Mister Galileo! Mister Galileo! How shall we stop him? Father Saturn is more powerful than I am.'

'Then we'll go to someone more powerful than Father Saturn,' said Mister Galileo.

Poor Mother Earth cried, 'Who is more powerful than Father Saturn?' and Mister Galileo answered, 'Our Lord the Sun.'

Mister Galileo went back to his garden and sat there till the Sun came up. The moment his glittering rays spread out like a crown on the edge of the sky, Mister Galileo stood up, raised his two hands, and cried, 'A word, my Lord, the Sun!'

'Be quick about it, then,' said the Sun. 'You know

as well as I do that if I change my course things will go wrong.'

Mister Galileo wasted neither breath nor time. 'Father Saturn is trying to steal our Moon,' he said.

'Is he really, Mister Galileo!'

'By this Shooting-Star, he is, my Lord!' cried Mister Galileo. He read the Star aloud to the Sun, and added, 'If the Moon changes her course, things will also go wrong.'

'Don't be afraid,' said the Sun. 'She shan't change her course.'

He rose higher and higher, till he was out of hearing. And Mister Galileo went to Mother Earth and told her she might rest easy, for the Sun had the matter in hand.

That night, when the Little Moon awoke, she found that she had been put back in her place; but the song of the Seven Moons still sang so sweetly in her mind, that she began once more to creep across the sky to Father Saturn far away. She had moved the billionth part of an inch, before a clear voice cried:

'Halt!'

She looked about her; all the sky seemed bare.

Then, quite close to the top of her crescent she spied a single star.

'Who are you?' she cried.

'Never mind my name,' said the bright speck. 'I am the Star chosen by our Lord the Sun to watch the Moon.'

'And why must I be watched?' cried the cross little Moon.

'Because you want to leave your Mother the Earth, and live in Father Saturn's ring of light.'

'What if I do?' said the Moon.

'If you do,' cried the Star, 'Heaven and Earth will crack.'

'Let them crack!' cried the Moon in a pet. 'I want to make silver patterns and sing sweet tunes, and play with my Seven Sisters in Saturn's House!' As she spoke, she shook herself, making the slightest movement out of her course; and Earth and Heaven shivered.

'Halt!' cried the Star.

And because the Sun had given him the power, he was too strong for her, and the Moon halted.

That is why, when she is a crescent, you will often see the Star that watches the Moon, shining near her, like a sentinel. For she wants what would hurt Heaven and Earth, and herself as well. Of course, she is still so young that she doesn't know any better.

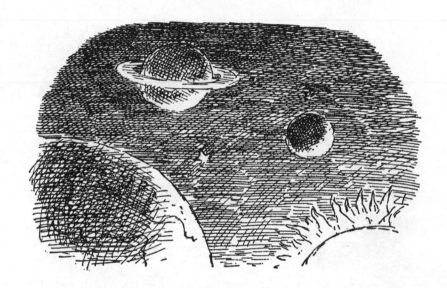

VIII

THE GREAT SEA-SERPENT

ONE bright April day Derry ran off to the Heath with his new boat under his arm. He was about to launch her on her first voyage across the pond. As he passed the corner, Jim sang out:

'What's the hurry?'

'I'm going to launch my boat,' shouted Derry.

'What's her name?'

'The *Rocking-horse,* of course.'

'Where's she bound for?

'Valparaiso!' shouted Derry.

'Well,' said Jim, 'don't stay there too long, for there's a squall blowing up.'

Derry couldn't see a speck or a sign of a squall; but Jim always knew. The good ship *Rocking-horse* had barely made her first trip across the pond, when the sky grew dark, the thunder rolled, and Derry had to scamper into shelter. The shower was short and sharp. As soon as the sky grew light again, Derry raced downhill, and the sun was already shining through the last of the rain when he reached the corner.

'Look out for rainbows!' called Jim cheerily, and pointed upwards with his stick. Derry saw a lovely arch of colour over the housetops; while he stared it grew brighter, and soon there was a second rainbow in the sky, reflected from the first.

'Is it true, Jim,' asked Derry, 'that there's a pot of gold buried at the foot of the rainbow?'

'I shouldn't wonder,' said Jim, stuffing his pipe. 'You see these gold rings in my ears?'

Derry had often admired and wondered at the

two gold rings Jim wore in his brown ears, and now he wondered more than ever, for Jim said, 'In a sort of a kind of a way, I got my gold rings off the end of a rainbow. Only it wasn't exactly a rainbow.'

'What was it then?' asked Derry.

'It was the Great Sea-Serpent,' said Jim.

'You haven't *seen* the Great Sea-Serpent, Jim!'

'With my own two eyes,' said Jim, 'and nobody else's.'

'Do tell!' begged Derry.

'There ain't a great deal to tell,' said Jim, 'though there was a very great deal of the Sea-Serpent. Now you sit still and listen.'

It was in the Indian Ocean. It happened after a thunder-shower no longer than the one we've just lived through, only forty times as heavy. As it cleared off, I looked out for rainbows, and there, to be sure, were two of them. Only ever so much brighter than the two up there. One of them was so bright, in fact, that I'd never seen the like of it before. It arched the sky from east to west, all violet-blue, and orange-yellow, and emerald-green, and ruby-red. It fair bedazzled the eye. So that when

I saw it give a wobble in the sky, I thought at first
my sight was playing me tricks.

But not at all! The rainbow went on wobbling.
Then it began to stretch itself; and next a great head
lifted up out of the western sea. Then I saw I'd been
mistaken. One of the rainbows was a real rainbow,
but the other one was the Great Sea-Serpent
himself.

He waved his head about in the air for a bit, and
then he let it down slowly, till his chin rested on my
knee. Was I afraid? Not a bit of it! That Sea-Serpent

had eyes as wistful as a dog's. One was blue and the other was green, and out of each of them a big tear rolled, and splashed on the deck.

'Hallo!' I said. 'What's the matter with *you*?'

The Sea-Serpent swallowed a sob and said, 'Nobody loves me.'

'How's that?' I asked.

'I'm too big,' said the Sea-Serpent.

'Stuff and nonsense!' I told him. 'Nothing's too big or too little to be loved. Look at babies.'

'Look at *me*,' sighed the Sea-Serpent. 'You can pet a little baby. But who could ever pet me?'

I began to feel sorry for the poor monster.

'Do you want to be petted?' I asked.

'More than anything,' said the Sea-Serpent.

'All right,' said I, '*I'll* pet you.'

'Oh, Jim!' said the Sea-Serpent joyfully; and he snuggled the tip of his snout against my chest.

'Hold hard!' I cried. 'Don't you start petting *me*, or there won't be any of me left!'

'I'll be good,' said the Sea-Serpent. 'Now begin.'

'What shall I begin with?' I asked.

'With my head,' said the Sea-Serpent.

Well, I began with his head, though it wasn't

very pettable, being all over knobs and bristles. However, I patted the knobs, and stroked between the bristles, and his eyes got sleepy with pleasure. He let out a sound between a hiss and a purr, like the sea washing the shore.

Presently he said, 'Thankee, Jim. That'll do for my head. Now get on a bit.'

I looked at him stretching up for miles and miles into the sky, and said, 'It's going to be a long job.'

'Never mind that,' said the Sea-Serpent. 'I want to be petted all over.'

'Move along, then,' I said. He shifted his head off my knee and laid it down on the deck at my feet; and he fetched a bit more of himself out of the sky, and flopped over my knees. I stroked and patted that bit too, and he went on purring and hissing in a way that made me drowsy.

Presently he said again, 'Thankee, Jim. *That* bit's done. Now for the next.' He coiled what I'd just petted round his head, and slid another length of himself across my lap. And I started patting and stroking all over again. And when he was satisfied, he coiled up *that* bit, and wriggled down some more of himself.

Well, I could go on telling you all day how I petted that Sea-Serpent, for there seemed to be no end to him. The coil on the deck got bigger and bigger, till I was afraid the *Rocking-horse* would sink under the weight, and *still* he kept on saying, 'Thankee, Jim!' and *still* kept on fetching himself down length after length.

I didn't know what to do. I wanted to please the poor chap, who had never been petted before. But my arm was beginning to ache. Yet I didn't like to stop in case he turned nasty, and if he turned nasty, well, he could swallow the *Rocking-horse* and all hands aboard as easy as you can swallow a peppermint drop.

Just as my arm got so tired that I thought I'd have to chance it, Cap'n Potts came out on the bridge. He'd been doing a bit of washing for himself, and as the sun was shining he began to peg it out on the rigging to dry. Before he pegged up a sock he gave it a last shake, and a spot of water fell on the Sea-Serpent on the deck below.

The Sea-Serpent gave a little shiver, and asked, 'What was that?'

'Drop o' wet,' said I, patting and stroking.

'Oh,' said the Sea-Serpent.

Then the Captain shook out his other sock, and a second spot fell on the Sea-Serpent below. He shivered again, and asked, 'What was *that*?'

'Another drop o' wet,' I said.

'Oh,' said the Sea-Serpent.

Then the Captain shook out his pyjamas, and a third drop fell. The Sea-Serpent gave a shudder that rocked the ship, and asked, 'How much more of it?'

'Quite a lot,' I said. I knew there was the Captain's vest still to come, and his pants, and his shirt, collar, and cuffs, and his bath-towel, and his table-napkin, and his pocket-handkerchief.

'Drat it!' said the Sea-Serpent. 'I came up for a little sun. But if it's going to rain again, I'm off! I never could stand the wet.'

With that he uncoiled himself, and began to slide across my knees at a tremendous rate. Down into the sea splashed his great head, while his thick, shining body slipped through my hands like greased lightning. Towards the finish it got thinner and thinner. When at last I got to the tail, it was no thicker than my finger, and on the very tip of it were

two gold rings. The tail whisked through my fists, leaving the rings behind it in my hands.

As soon as I let go of the Sea-Serpent's tail, it flicked right up into the air, past the Captain on the bridge. Cap'n Potts took it for a bit of the line, and pegged his Sunday shirt on to the end of it. Last thing I saw was the shirt disappearing into the sea, as the Captain stepped down from the bridge.

'Did you see that rainbow, Jim?' he asked.

I looked up at the sky. There wasn't a sign of the

Great Sea-Serpent, only the real rainbow fading away as hard as it could fade.

'I did,' I said, 'and I shall never see a rainbow the like o' *that* again.'

'And what have you got there?' asked Cap'n Potts, staring at the rings in my hands.

'These?' I said. 'Oh, these came out of the pot of gold at the rainbow's end.'

'I see,' said Cap'n Potts. 'Some people are born lucky.'

I agreed with him, and hung the two rings in my ears; and they are the rings you see there today. Other seamen may wear rings out of the jeweller's shop; but *my* ear-rings came off the Great Sea-Serpent's tail.

IX

CHIMMAPANZY AND POLLYMALLOY

'Hot?' said Jim. 'Yes, you may *call* this hot, if you like.'

He wiped his streaming forehead as he spoke, and Derry thought Jim looked very hot indeed. It was the hottest day Derry himself had ever known. The pavement burned through the soles of his sandals;

he only wore a white shirt and shorts, and they were wringing wet, because he was perspiring so. He sat down on the shady side of the orange-box, and looked admiringly at Jim. If Jim didn't call this hot, what did he call hot?

Derry asked it, aloud. 'What *do* you call hot, Jim?'

'I call the Island of Bungaloo hot,' said Jim.

'Where's that?' asked Derry.

Jim shut one eye and tapped his forehead. 'I couldn't say exactly *where* it is. It was somewhere in the South Seas. The *Rocking-horse* was cruising there at the time. One night a tornado blew along, turned the ship round seven times, and dropped her. In the morning Cap'n Potts didn't know where he was at all. That tornado had set us down in a place that was strange to us.

'We were cast up on a shore of silver sand. The sea-water was as blue as your Ma's sapphire ring; it splashed in and out of a coral reef growing out of the ocean like red-and-white trees. The shore was strewn with oyster-shells full of pearls, and purple starfish; and there were little rose-pink crabs scuttling about, and green jelly-fish shining in the sun.

Beyond the beach was a jungle of banana trees. And the sun was hotter than it is anywhere else on earth. That was the Island of Bungaloo.'

'How did you know it was called Bungaloo?' asked Derry.

'Because a Cockatoo sat on a banana tree and said so. *"Bungaloo!"* she screeched. *"Bungaloo! Illa-illa-illa-Bungaloo!"* So then of course we knew.'

'Perhaps she wasn't saying the name of the Island at all,' persisted Derry. 'Perhaps she was just saying, "What good bananas!"'

'The Bungaloose for a good banana is Bonnabanana,' said Jim. 'And the Bungaloose for a bad banana is Baddabanana! And if you're telling this story, *you* can tell it, but if I'm telling it, *I'll* tell it, and which is it to be?'

'You tell it, Jim,' said Derry.

Very well then! We asked the Cockatoo her name, and she said *'Pollymalloy!'* Then Cap'n Potts said, 'What shall we have for breakfast, Pollymalloy?' And that Cockatoo picked a big bunch of bananas and started handing them round. By the time it came to me, they were all gone, so I tweaked her tail a little too hard. At that she reared her crest at me, screeching, '*Jimmajumbo! Badda Jimmajumbo!*' After that she took a dislike to me.

Everybody else made a great pet of her, as sailors will of any living creature. And Pollymalloy was pleasant to them all. Cap'n Potts was her favourite, and she'd kow-tow with the Mate and hob-nob with the Cook as though she'd known them in their cradles. But me? Oh, no! Whenever she got the chance she tweaked my hair with her strong, curved beak, like iron. She ruffled her crest at me, she flapped her wings at me, she screeched '*Badda Jimmajumbo!*' till I got the headache. And worst of all, she stole my bananas.

I could *not* keep my breakfast or my dinner from her wicked claws, and when I complained to the Captain, he only laughed. Pollymalloy was such a pet with him and the crew that they all took her part.

I'm sorry to say this put me in the sulks. I took my bananas to the other end of the beach, and sat and ate by myself, and when my mates called to me, I wouldn't answer.

'Jim's lost his tongue, boys!' said Cap'n Potts.

That made me sulkier than ever, and I decided not to speak to them at all. I kept it up for two days, and it was dull work. But you know what the sulks are; once you start sulking you don't know how to stop, even if you want to. So I thought, 'This isn't good enough. As I can't bring myself to speak to my mates, I'll go into the banana jungle and live by myself.' And I took myself off, in a fit of temper, on the hottest day of the year.

The banana jungle was like an oven. I pushed my way through it, and felt as though I was being cooked. Presently I pushed right through it, and found the sea again on the other side. When I saw that shining water, I could hardly wait to pull off my clothes and plunge in, and when I was in it I could hardly bear to come out.

I stayed swimming about in it for the best part of the day. Then by accident I swallowed a jelly-fish through keeping my mouth open a bit too wide. It stuck in my throat, and I could *not* spit it out.

I got out of the sea, and stood on the beach, trying to cough the jelly-fish up. But the obstinate thing wouldn't budge. I could not cough it up, and I could not gulp it down. And when I tried to say

what I thought about it, I could not make a single
sound but '*Gug-gug-gug!*'

That didn't matter, because I'd nobody to talk to.
I made the best of a bad job, and started looking
round for my clothes. And my clothes were nowhere to be seen.

Well, *that* didn't matter either, seeing how hot it
was. I picked some banana leaves and dressed myself up a bit, and then I began to want my supper.
I thought if I swallowed a banana it might push the
jelly-fish down.

Just as I started peeling one, I heard a sound in the
jungle behind me, and when I looked up, what do
you think I saw? I saw myself coming out from
behind a tree!

At least, it was somebody very like me, dressed
in my own clothes. I tried to say, 'Hallo, mate! What
are you doing in my trousers?' But all that came out
was '*Gug-gug-gug!*'

The stranger ambled up to me, and then I saw it
was not a man, but a great big Chimpanzee. He
seemed very pleased with himself, and he was
actually smoking my own pipe filled with my own
baccy.

G

We looked each other up and down, and suddenly
he tucked his arm in mine, and began to strut about
as pleased as though he'd found his long-lost brother.
To tell the truth, I'd grown so hairy on the voyage
that we did look very much alike.

'What a lark it would be,' I thought, 'to take the
old chap back to Cap'n Potts just as he is, dressed up
in my togs.' For somehow my swim in the sea had
washed the sulks out of me, and I wanted nothing
better than to go back and make it up with my
mates and Pollymalloy.

So I and the Chimpanzee set off through the banana trees, and reached the other shore just as Cap'n Potts was ladling out the oyster stew for supper.

'Hallo,' he said, 'here's Jim. But what's that he's got with him?'

Everybody looked at us and burst out laughing. Then I tried to tell them all about it, but of course the only thing I could say was *'Gug-gug-gug!'* which made them laugh still more.

Then the Chimpanzee walked up to the fire where the oyster stew was cooking. The men were eating it out of coconut shells, and that Chimpanzee picked up a shell and held it out for some stew. No sooner was it filled than Pollymalloy flew out of a tree and upset it. She started screeching at the Chimpanzee, *'Jimmajumbo! Badda Jimmajumbo!'*

It amused me very much to see that Pollymalloy thought the Chimpanzee was me. He jumped up, threw his coconut shell at her, and began to talk back. And all he said was *'Gug-gug-gug!'*

'Ha, ha!' said Cap'n Potts; 'Jim's lost his tongue still.'

'Poor old Jim!' said Cookie to the Chimpanzee,

'Come along and have some more stew.' He made the Chimp sit down by the fire, and gave him another helping.

Well, that amused me too. But suddenly the Captain said, 'What are we going to do with that ugly old Chimpanzee?' and as he said it he looked straight at me. 'He looks dangerous,' said Cap'n Potts, 'and we'll tie him up out of harm's way.'

That didn't amuse me quite so much. I thought it was time to explain things, and tried to say, 'Here, mates, *I'm* Jim, and *that's* the Chimpanzee dressed up in my clothes.' But that jelly-fish was still stuck in my throat, so naturally all that came out was '*Gug-gug-gug!*'

Everybody laughed at me. The more they laughed the more I tried to speak, and the more I tried to speak the more they laughed.

They got a rope and tied me to a tree, and gave me a coconut, which not being a Chimpanzee of course I couldn't crack. I longed for oyster stew, but they never thought of giving me that. Chimpanzees aren't supposed to eat oyster stew. I gave up all hopes that they would find out their mistake, because Pollymalloy kept flying first at the Chimpanzee, screeching *'Jimmajumbo! Jimmajumbo!'* and then at me, screeching, *'Chimmapanzy! Chimmapanzy!'*

If you ask me, she knew which was which all the time, and mixed us up out of spite.

As for Chimmapanzy, he entered into the joke thoroughly. He ate his meal like a Christian, and he smoked his pipe; and after supper when Cookie got out his concertina and started playing, up jumped Chimmapanzy and danced a hornpipe.

Cap'n Potts clapped his hands. 'Bravo, Jim!' he cried; and all the crew followed suit. It made me sick.

That night Chimmapanzy slept on the beach under my blanket, like a man, and I had to sleep up the tree like a monkey.

Next morning that tornado turned up again out of nowhere. Cap'n Potts saw her coming through his telescope, and said, 'Mates, we'll go aboard, for if we don't the *Rocking-horse* will blow off without us.'

'What about Pollymalloy and Chimmapanzy?' asked Cookie.

'Oh,' said Cap'n Potts, 'we'll take them along.'

I was glad of that, for I didn't want to be left high and dry in Bungaloo, while Chimmapanzy sailed in my place. We all went aboard together, and the Captain said, I'll have Pollymalloy in my cabin, and Jim shall share his bunk with Chimmapanzy. Neither of em says anything but *Gug-gug-gug,* so they'll be good company for each other.'

Then he led me to my own bunk, and said, 'Shake down there, Chimmapanzy. And to Chimmapanzy he said, 'Come along, Jim, and help to haul the anchor.'

I fair hated not working along with my mates, and Chimmapanzy grinned at me as though he knew it. Off he went with Cap'n Potts and I was left alone. I was very sad at the fate that had come upon me. I did not wish to spend the rest of my life as a chimpanzee.

Soon the tornado was upon us. It picked up the *Rocking-horse,* turned her round seven times, and dropped her. The *Rocking-horse* fell with such a bump, that it made me cough as I'd never coughed before.

While I was coughing, the cabin door burst open, and in tottered Chimmapanzy. I hardly knew him again. His eyes were rolling in his head, he was

clasping his stomach with his hands, and, believe me
or not, he looked *green*. I knew at once what was
the matter; he was sea-sick. You couldn't expect any
chimpanzee to get his sea-legs in a tornado like that.
But Chimmapanzy wasn't waiting to get his sea-
legs. He tottered up to the bunk, tore off his clothes,
pulled me out of the bunk, and dressed me up in my
own things again. I was still coughing.

When he'd done dressing me, Chimmapanzy
rushed up on the deck, and I rushed after him—still
coughing.

I was just in time to see him dive overboard into

the tossing sea, where he swam as fast as he could for the Island of Bungaloo. I went on coughing.

The sailors gave a shout. Cookie cried, 'Look, mates! Chimmapanzy's got away from us.' Then he turned to me and said, 'Jim, you lubber, why did you let him escape?'

It did me good, I can tell you, to hear myself called by my own name again. I gave a last cough, and out popped the jelly-fish, and flopped upon the deck. Then I cleared my throat and answered, 'I let Chimmapanzy go because he was sick. He was sicker than any man I ever saw. I would not be so cruel as to make a prisoner of the poor dumb beast.'

'Poor dumb beast, eh?' said Cookie. '*Gug-gug-gug!*' And he winked at me as he said it.

Then all the crew, including Cap'n Potts, winked too. And I saw that they'd known which was which all the time, and had played the joke on me to pay me out for my sulks.

And if ever I showed sulky again, somebody would be sure to gurgle '*Gug-gug-gug!*' That would make me laugh, and I'd be cured. For once you've started laughing, you can't go on sulking. It's the law of nature.

X

JIM SMELLS THE SEA

IT was a hot, dusty day, and London seemed deserted. For it was the tenth of August, and everybody was out of town. Jim sat at his corner feeling lonely, for he had nobody to talk to. The children he knew and loved had gone away to the sea, or the farms, or the hills, or the woods. He missed them badly; and most of all, he missed Derry.

Presently the Postman came along to open the pillar-box.

'Hallo, Jim,' he said cheerily. 'All by yourself?'

'That's it,' said Jim.

The Postman stuffed his sack with the letters in the box, locked the red door again, and went away. Jim sat very still on his orange-box, his old hands pressed on the knob of his stick. He stared along the empty street, thinking of his many years; for it was his birthday, and he was eighty years old. Presently his head nodded, fell forward on his chest, and Jim dozed.

In his doze he dreamed about things he had seen and places he had been to: of the good ship *Rocking-horse,* and Cap'n Potts and Cookie. He dreamed of the farm he had been born on, and the rooks in the elm-trees, and the Great Sea-Serpent, and Polly-malloy. He dreamed of Flip the Penguin, of the Green Kitten, of the Parrot-Man, and of Mister Galileo who knew all; of castor-oil and Claude the Codfish, of Chimmapanzy and the banana-trees of Bungaloo. All these, and many more things, old

Jim dreamed of; and presently he dreamed of Derry running down the street, of Derry throwing his arms round his neck, of Derry clapping a shell to his ear, and crying:

'Happy birthday, Jim! Listen to the sea! Many Happy Returns of the Day!'

Jim woke with a start, and rubbed his eyes. Was he dreaming still? For there *was* Derry, dancing about him excitedly, crying, 'Happy birthday, Jim, happy birthday!' And there *was* a shell clapped against his ear, the very shell he had given Derry on *his* birthday and in it he could hear the wash of the sea.

'Bless my buttons!' cried Jim. 'What's the meaning of this? You're at the seaside, you are, not in town!'

'Yes, I know,' said Derry. 'I *am* at the seaside really, but Daddy drove me up to wish you Many Happy Returns of the Day.'

Jim stared at Derry's Daddy's motor-car standing in the road, with Derry's Daddy smiling inside. Jim beamed and touched his hat, 'That's very kind of Mr. Vane. *Our* hat, sir!'

'And,' Derry went on, 'to drive you back to the sea with us.'

'Me!' cried Jim.

'Because,' explained Derry, 'you're eighty today, and you said you'd rather have a smell of the sea on your birthday than any other present.'

Jim's beam became so big and broad that it spread all over his face. Then it suddenly crinkled up, and it looked as if he was going to cry.

Derry's Daddy jumped out of the car and clapped him on the back, 'Hurry up, Jim; we ought to be back in time for tea. Derry has got it all arranged, and you're to stay for a fortnight in the cottage of the lifeboat man.'

'He's a very good sailor,' said Derry, 'but he hasn't been to so many places as you have, and doesn't know as many stories.'

'Once let me smell the sea again,' said Jim, 'and I'll tell you more stories than I've ever told you yet.'

'Hop in,' said Derry's Daddy.

Jim got up slowly, leaning on his stick. He climbed into the big motor-car and Derry got in beside him. Away they whizzed; and by tea-time Jim was looking at the sea with all his eyes, and listening to the sea with all his ears, and smelling at the sea with all his nose.

While the orange-box stood at the corner of the street all by itself.